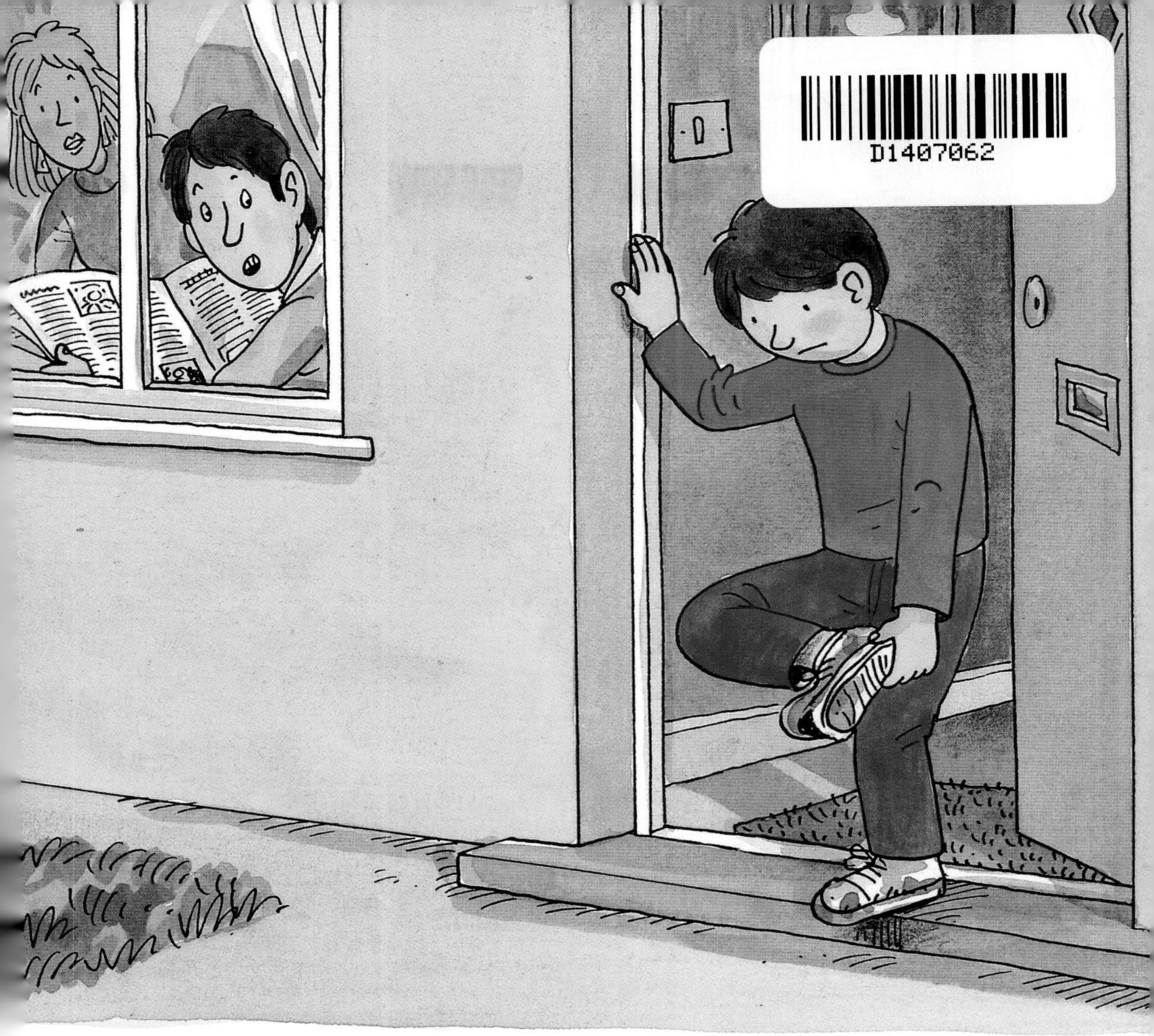

Chip wanted new trainers.

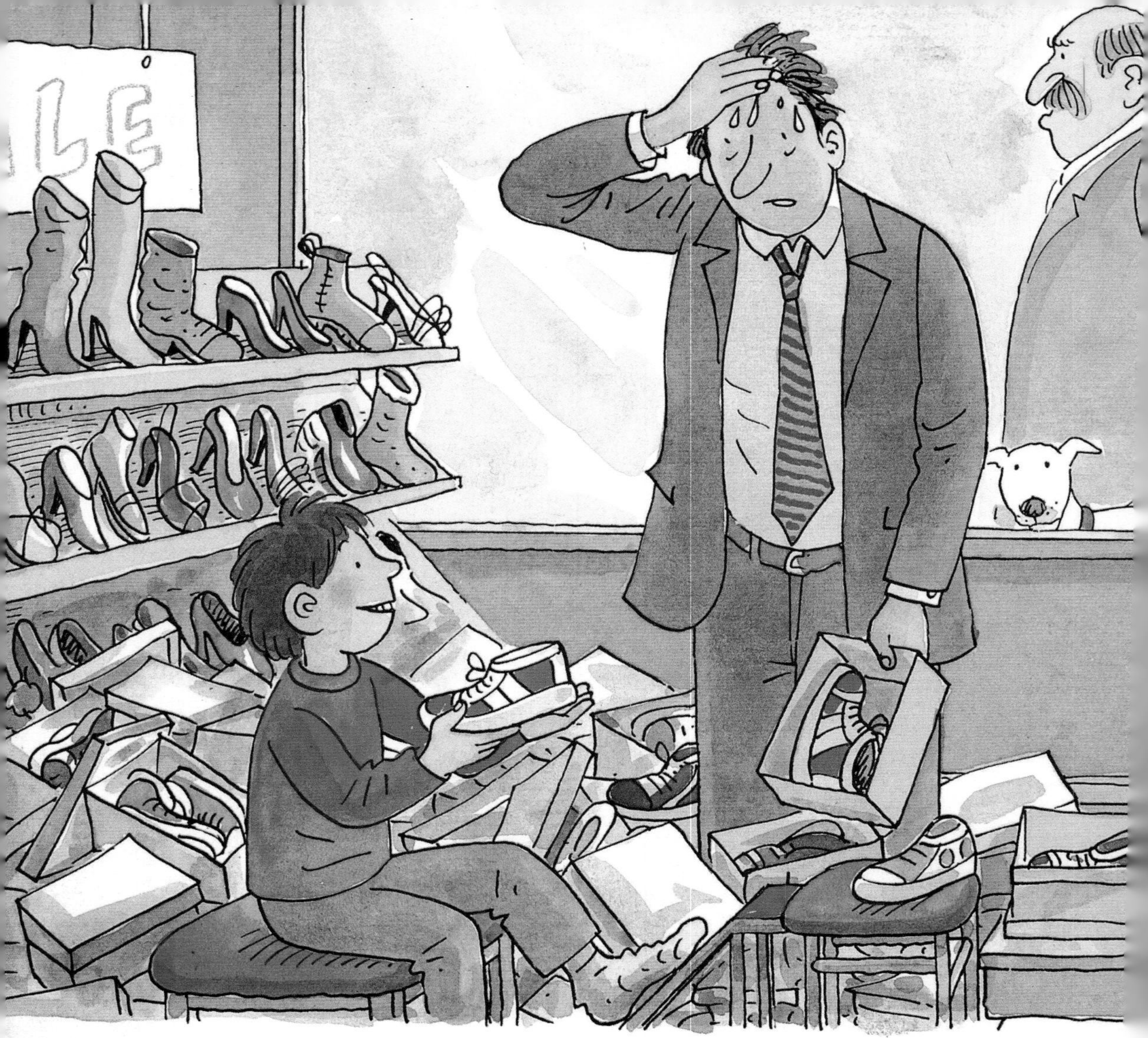

He liked this pair.

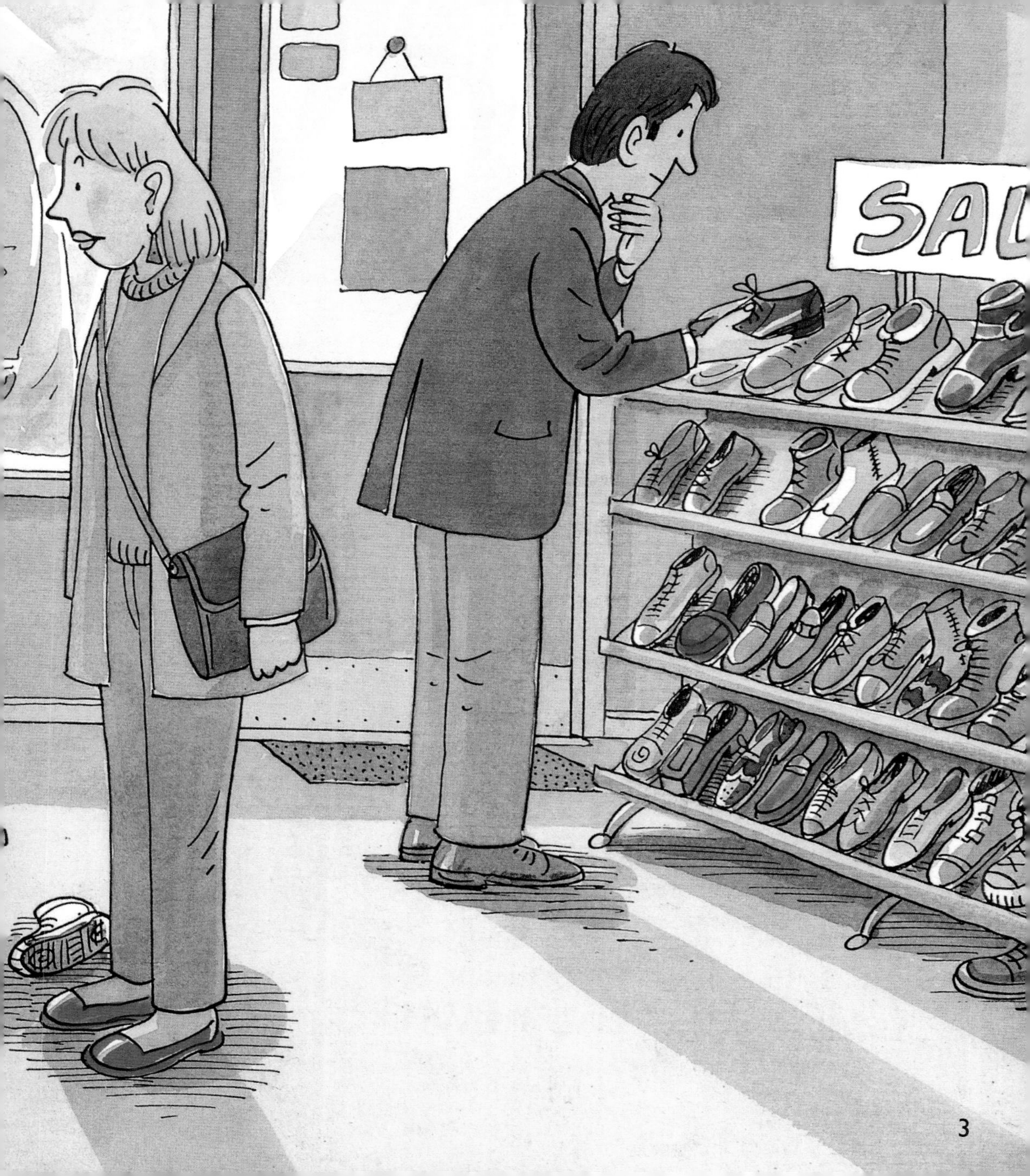
SAL

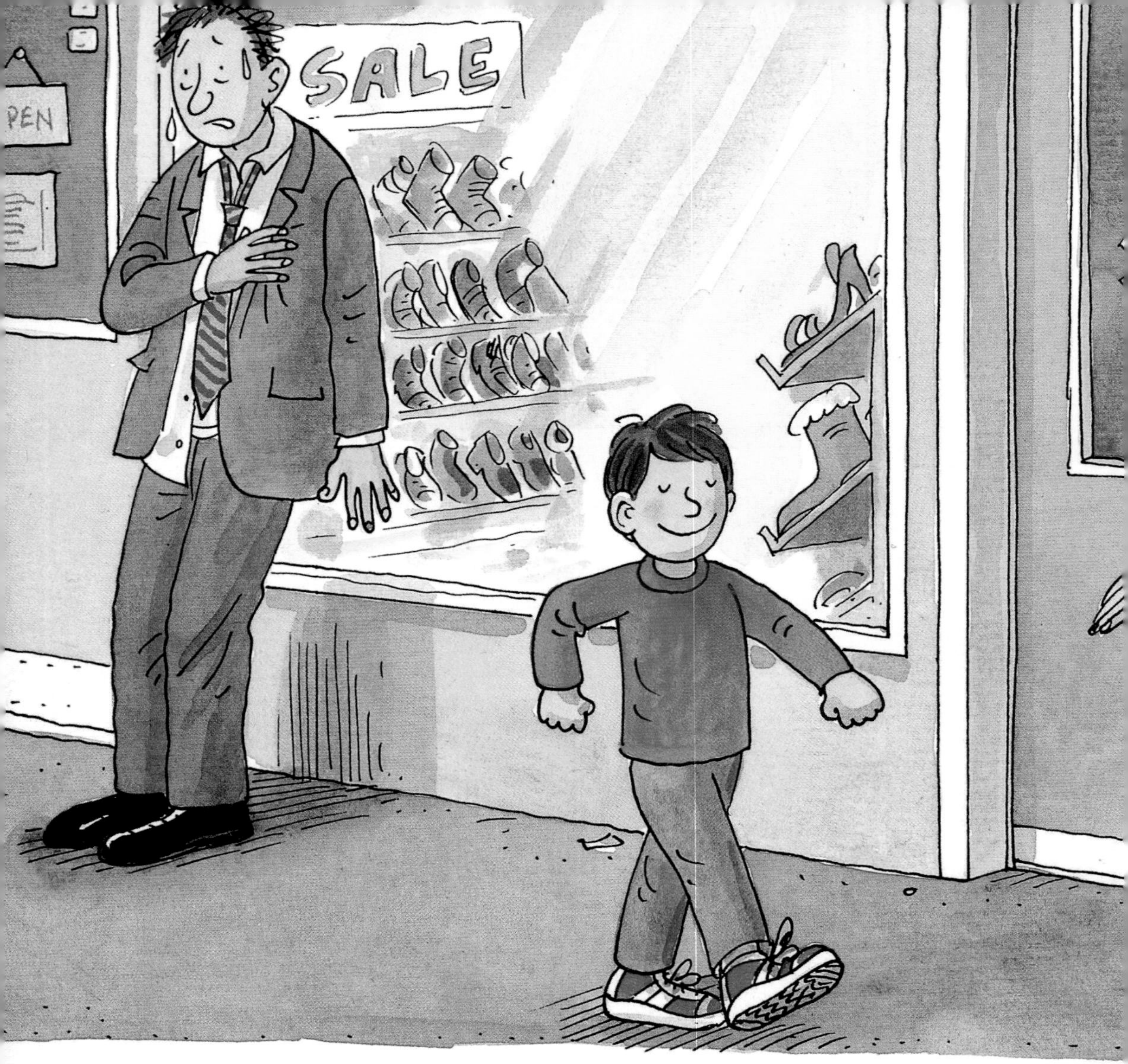

Chip wore the new trainers.

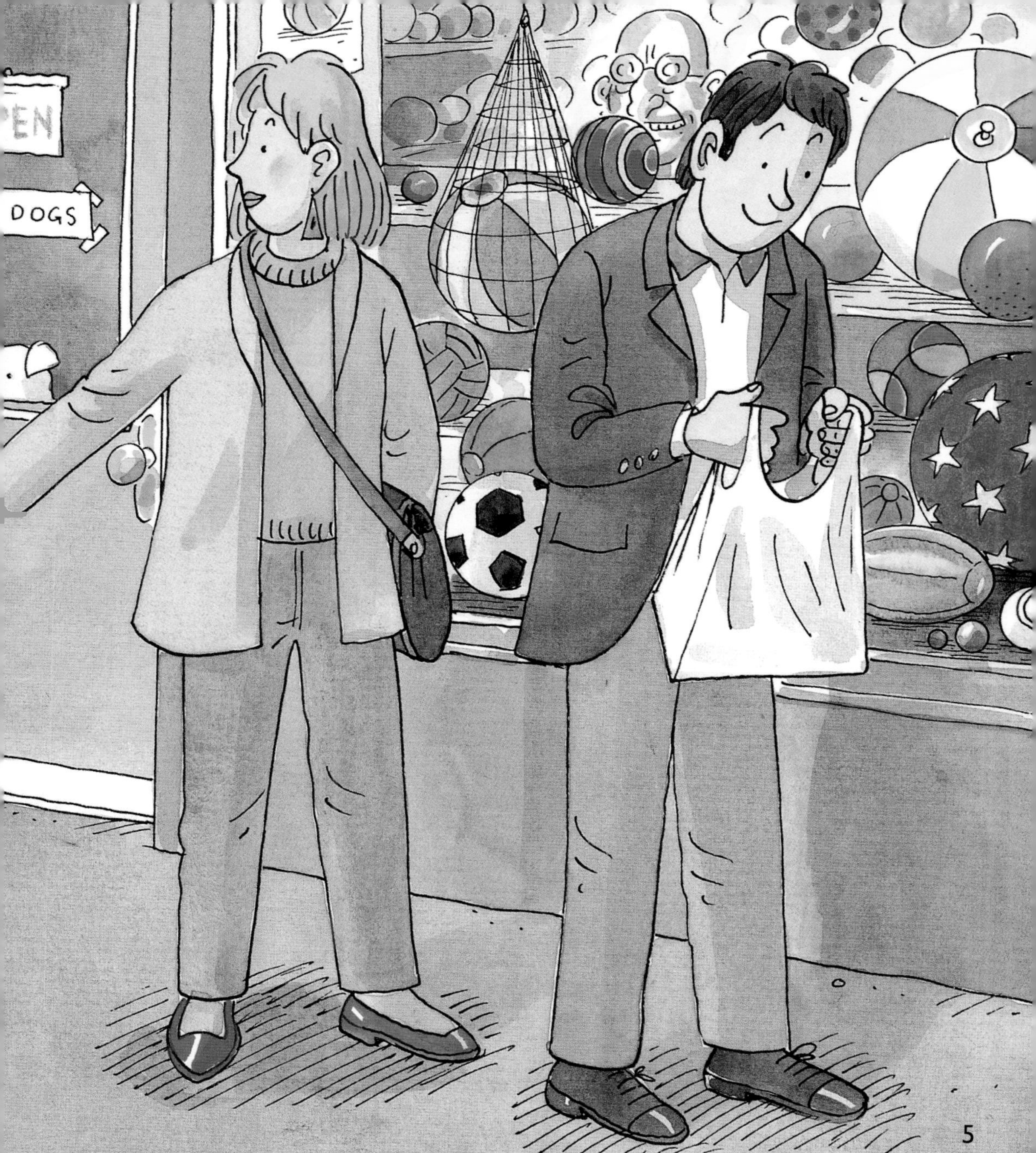
PEN
DOGS

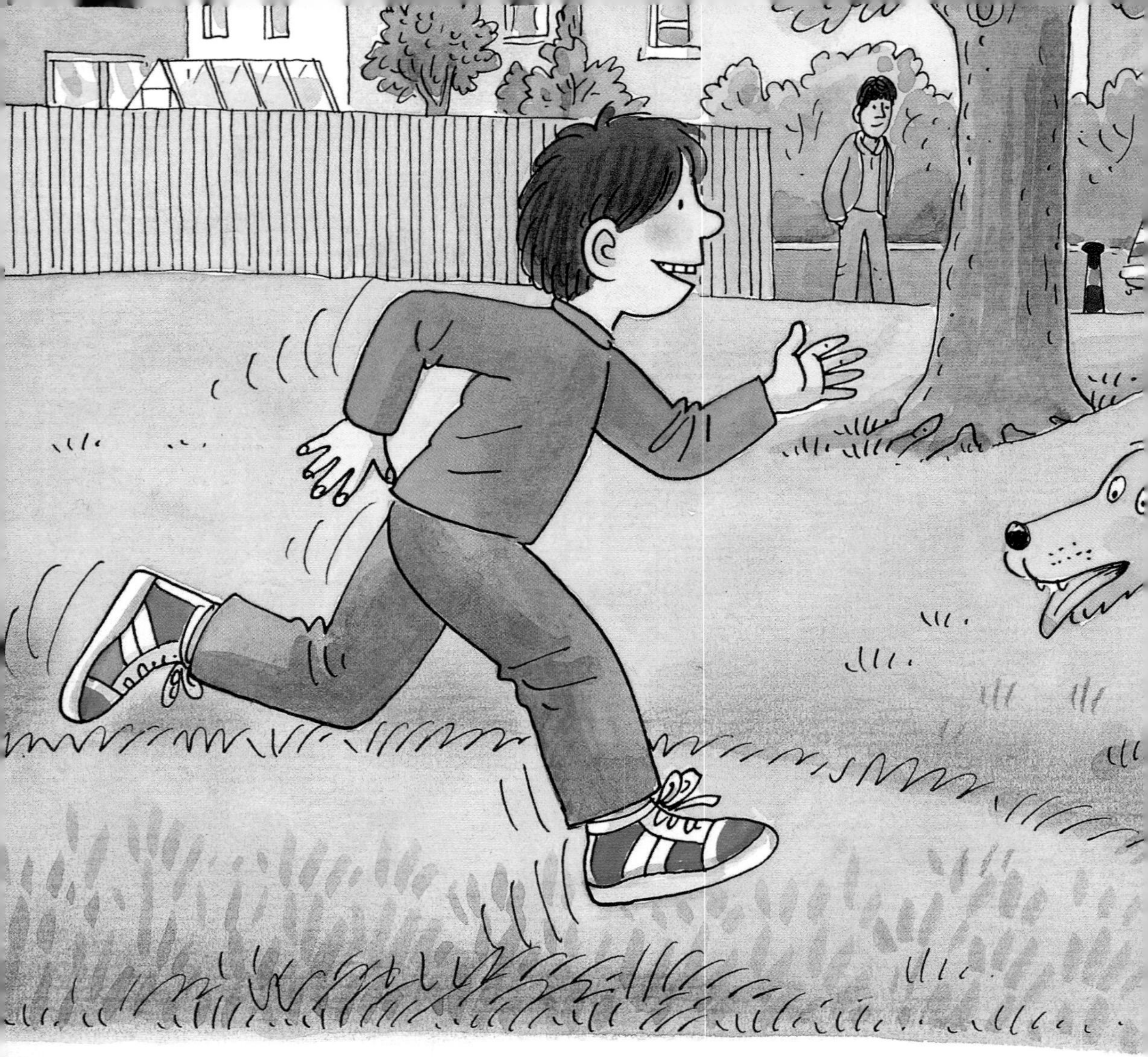

Chip went to play.

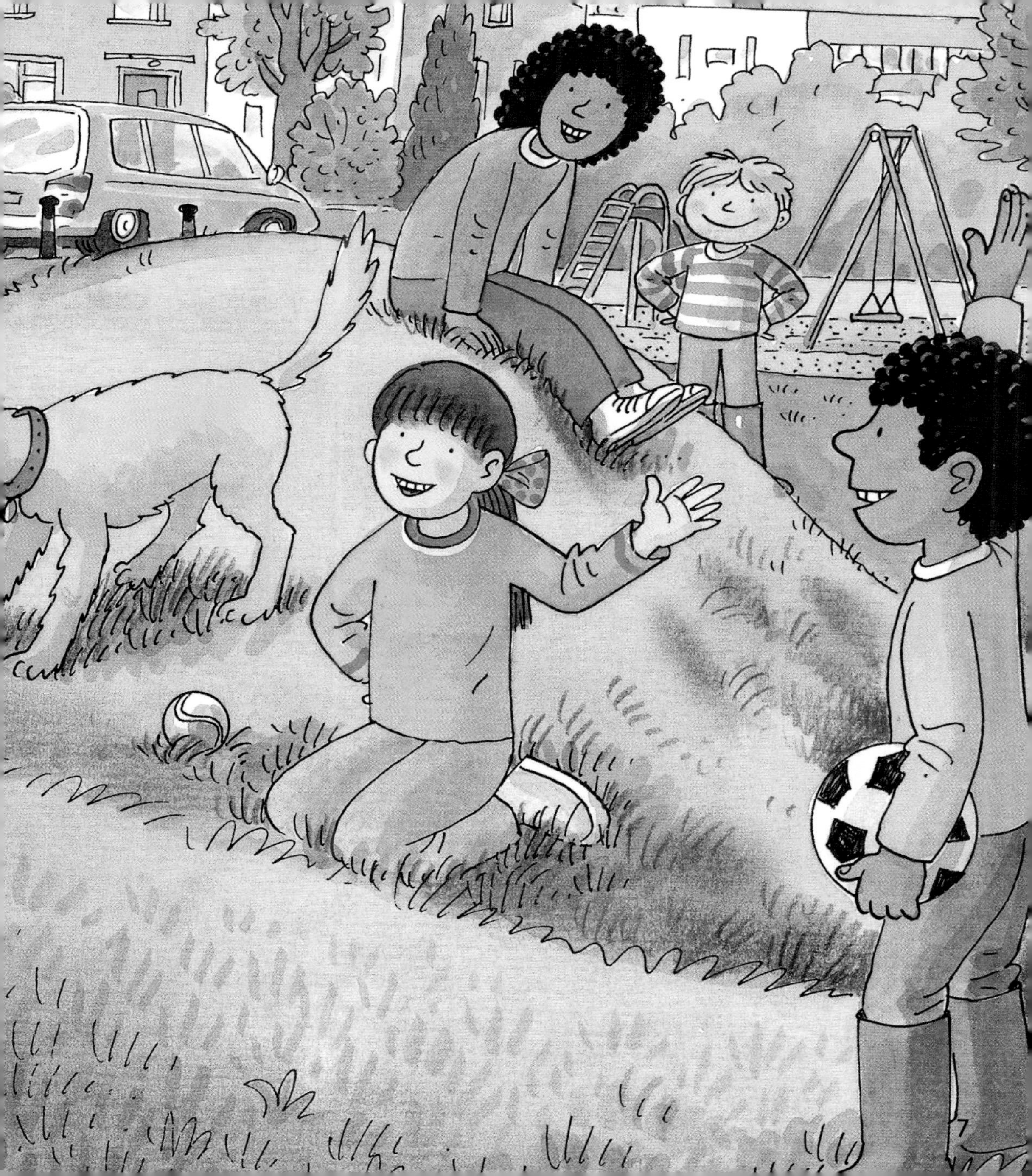

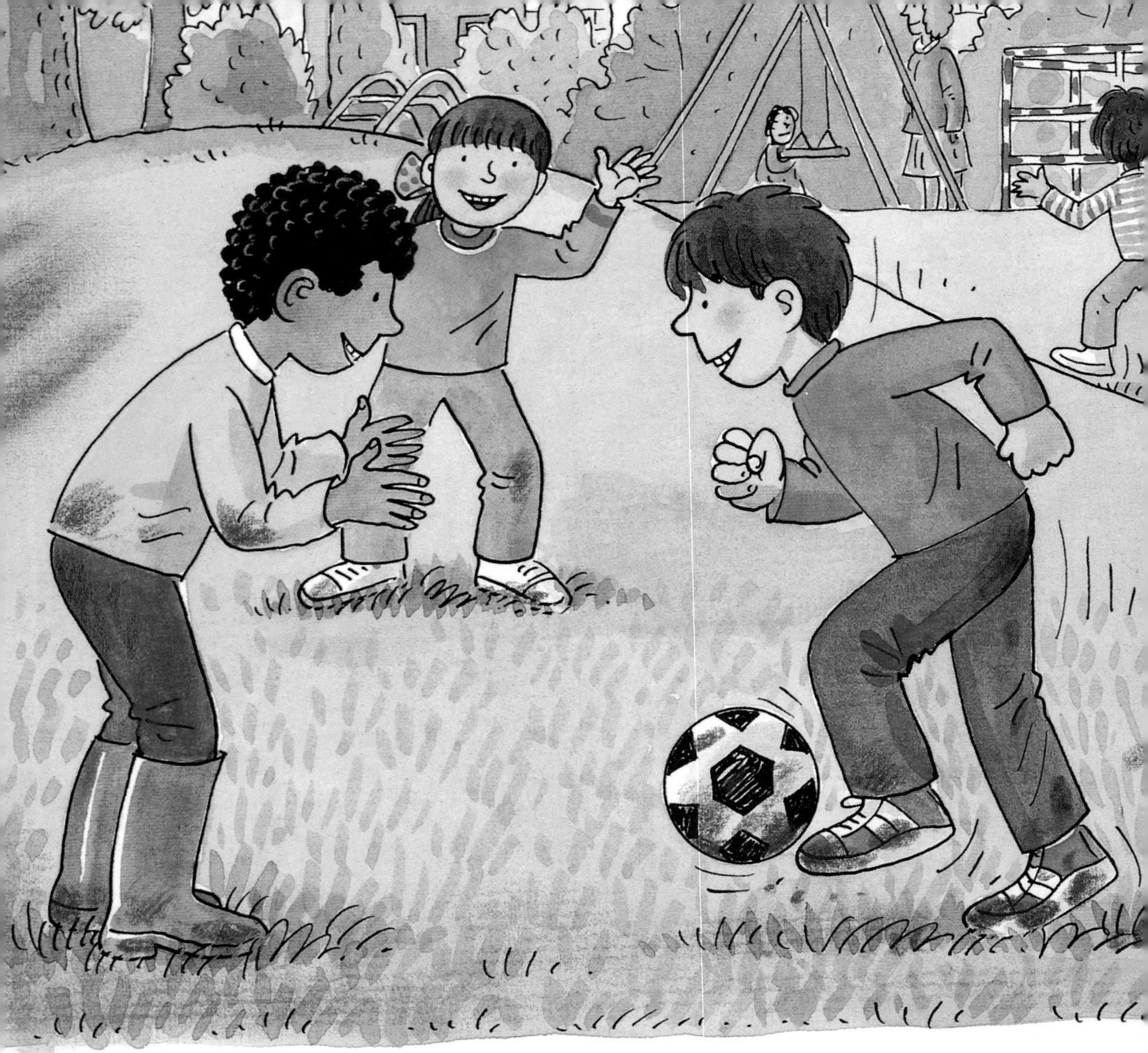

The trainers got muddy.

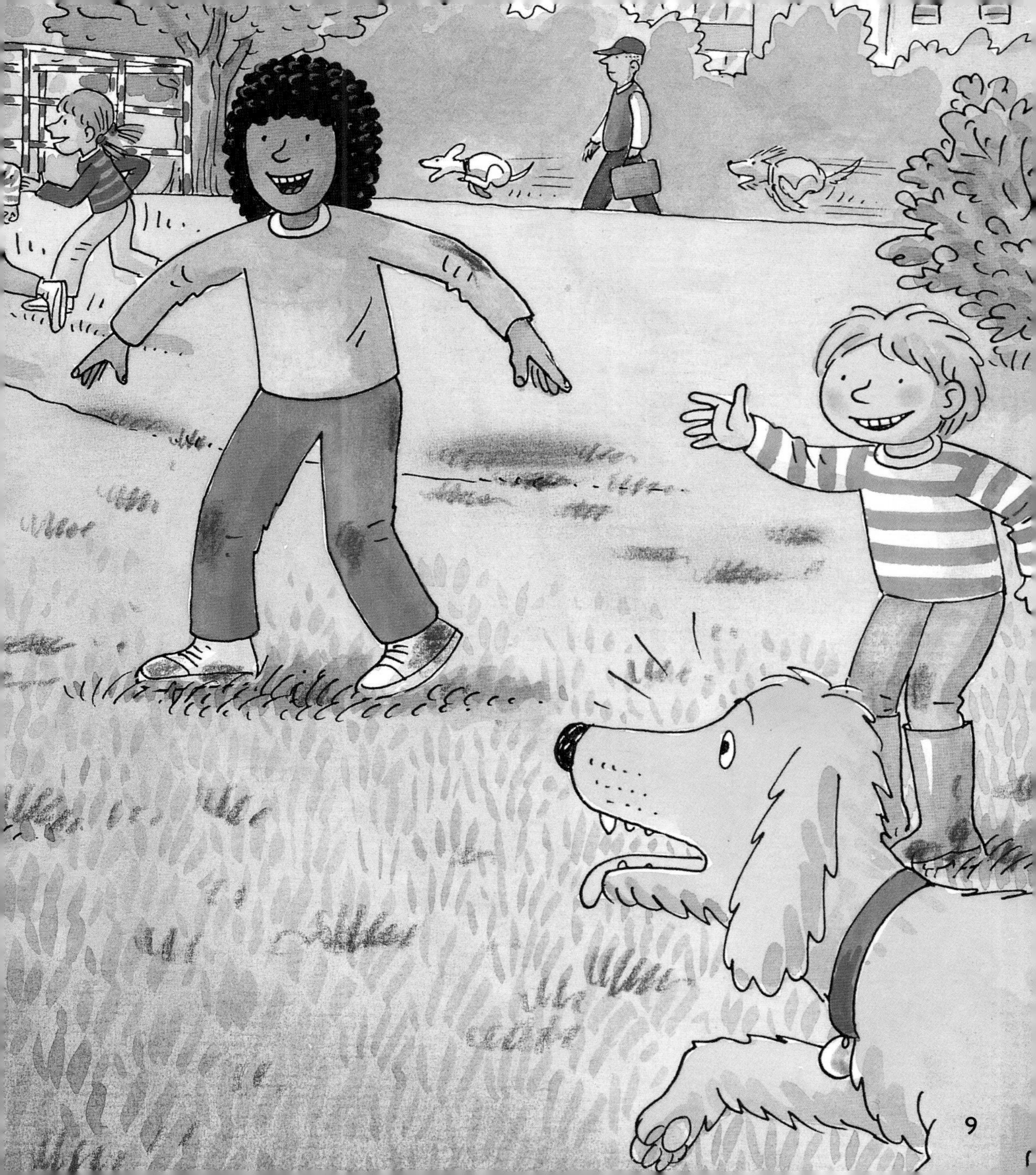

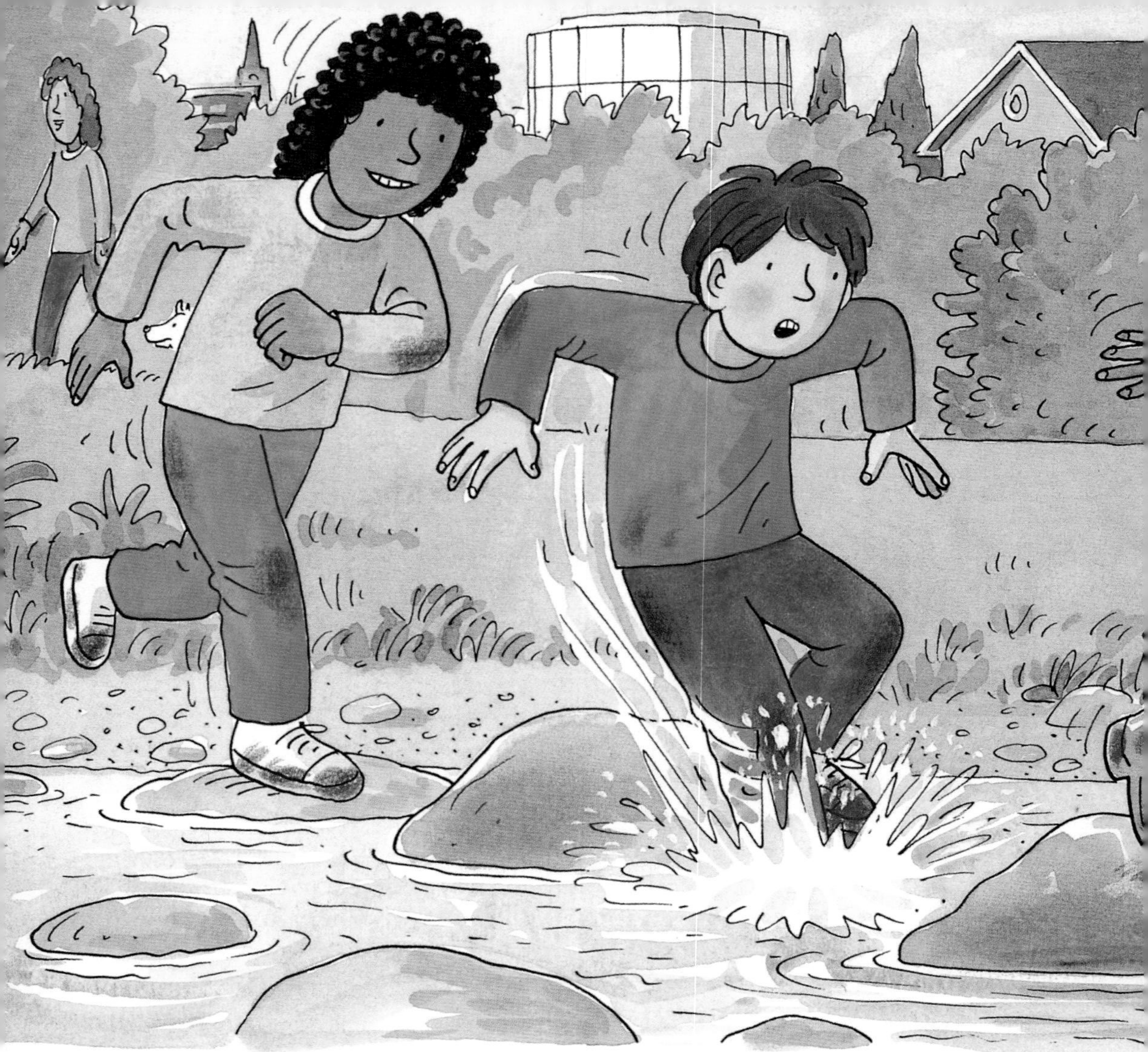

The trainers got wet.

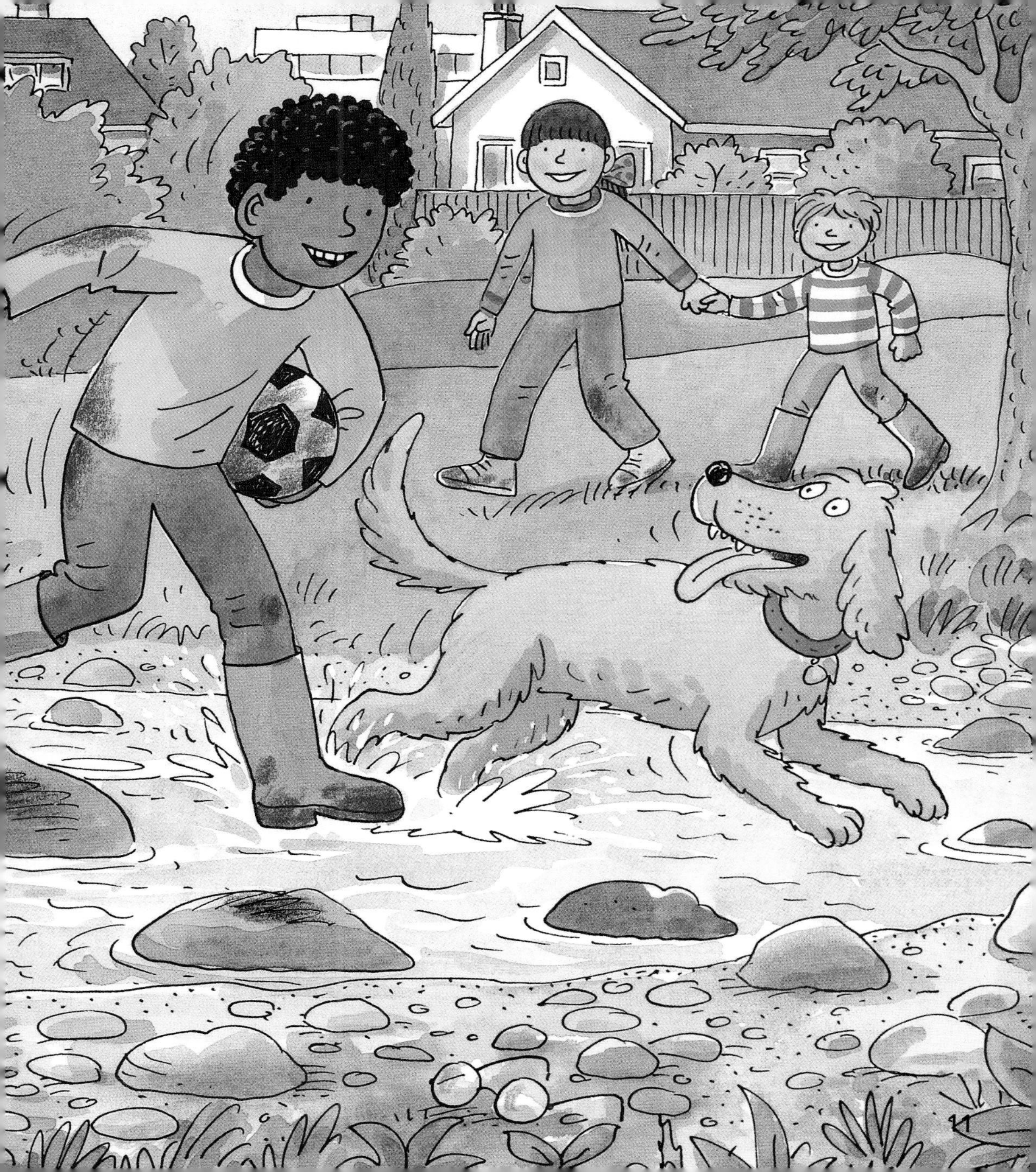

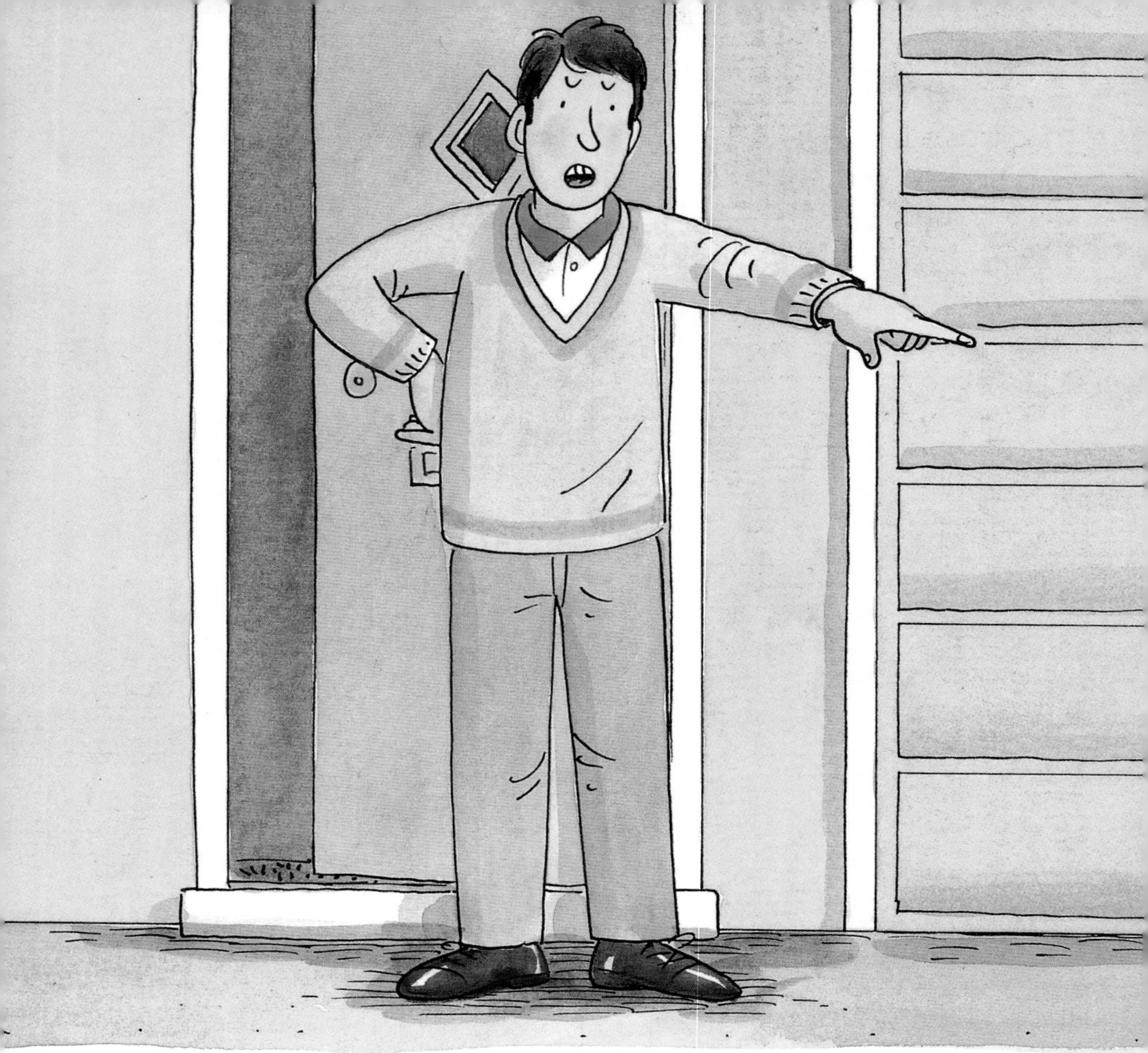

Dad was cross.

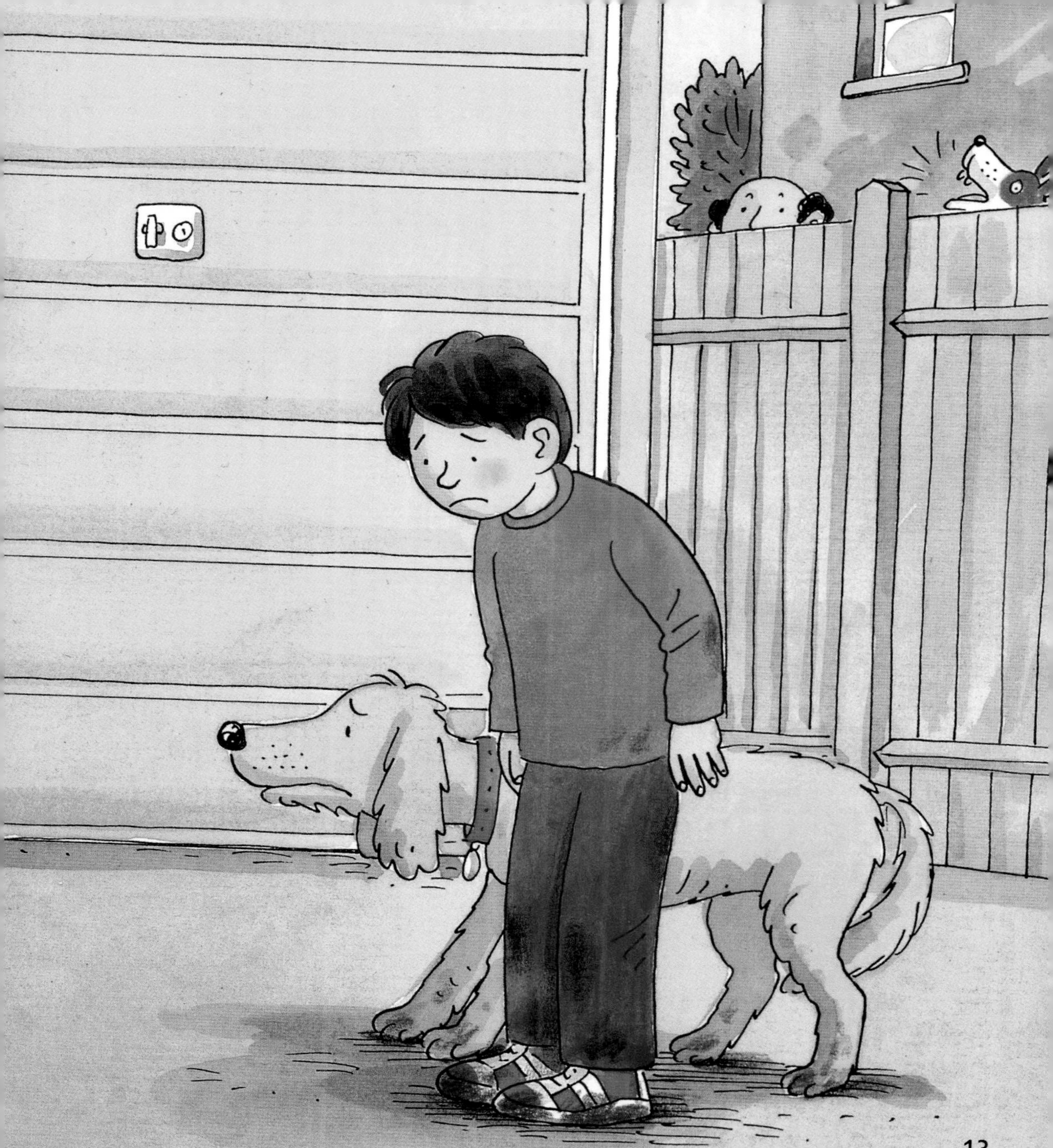

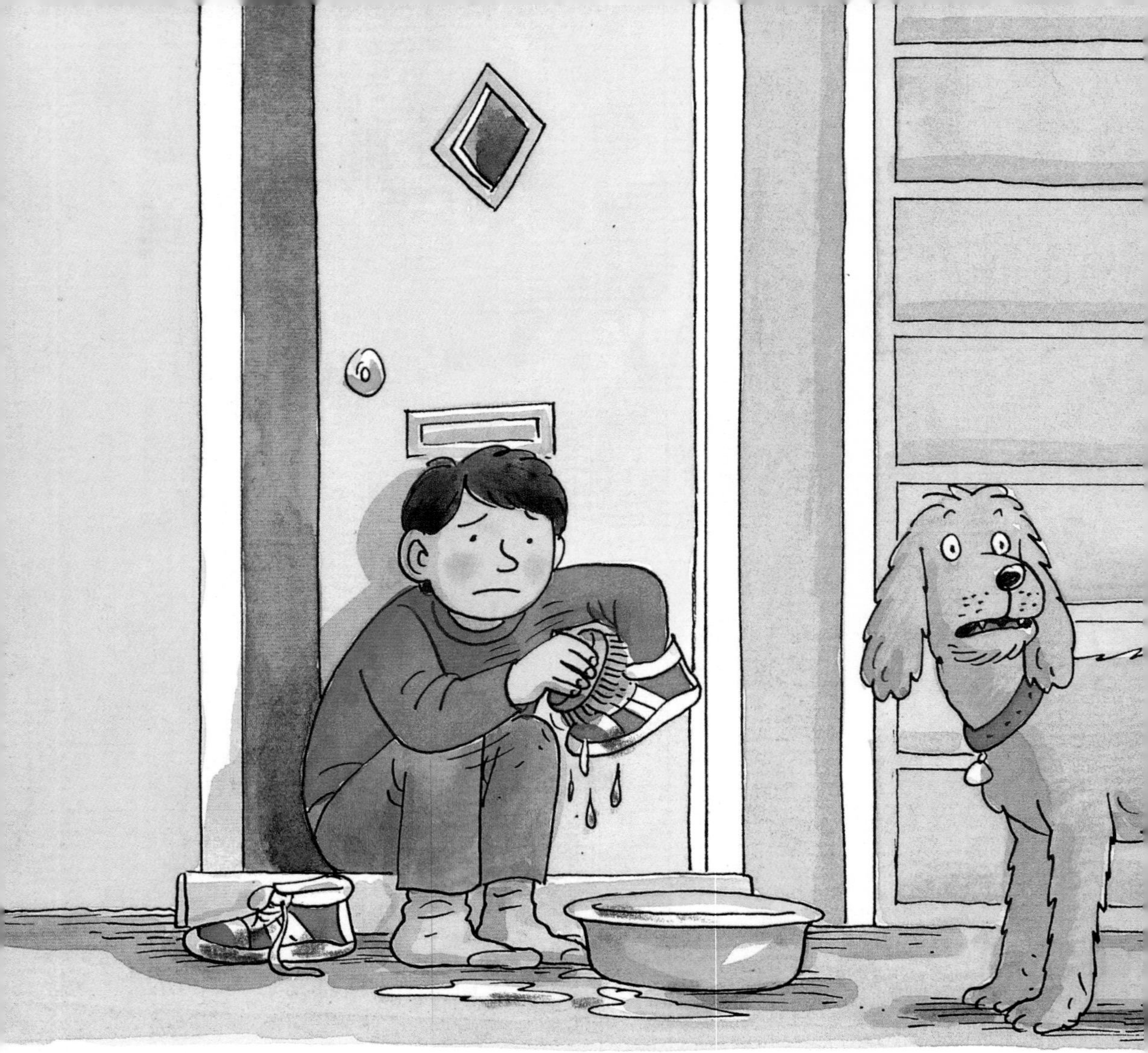

Chip washed the trainers.

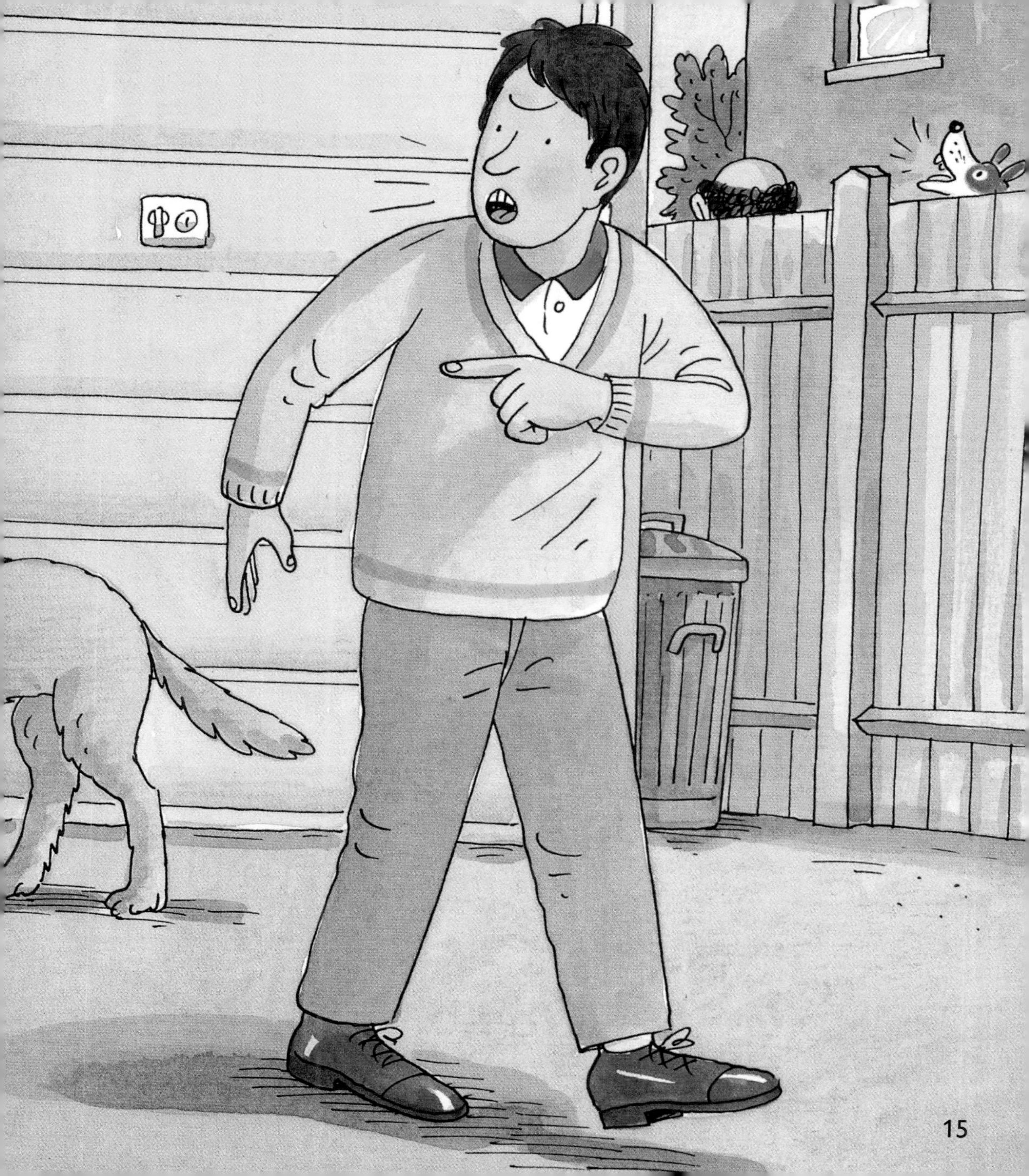

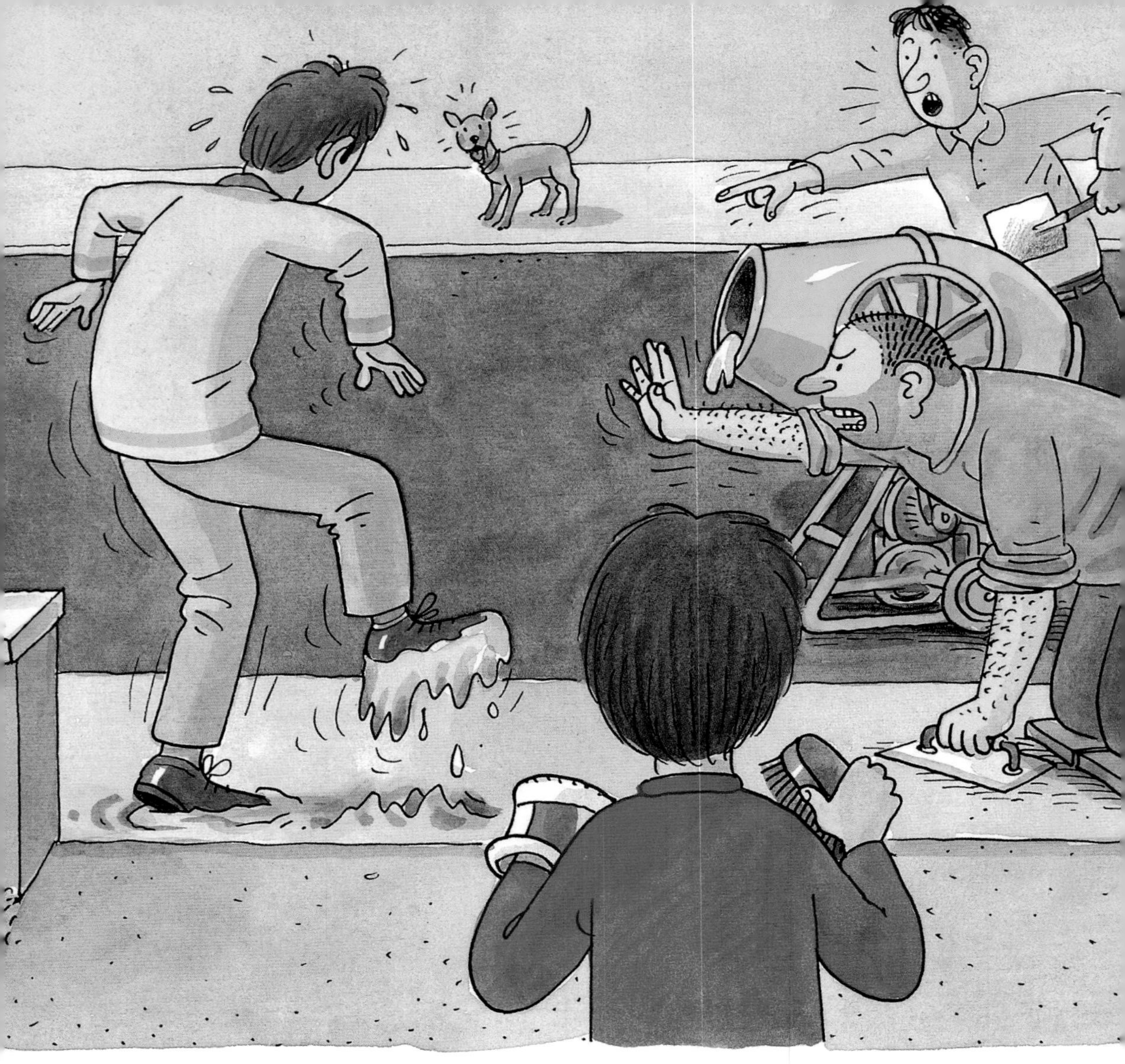

Oh no!